For my daughter Esme- I hope your imaginati⸺⸺ continues to grow.

To my husband Tremaine- Thank you for en⸺ write. Without you, this would not hav⸺

Copyright © 2022 Jennifer Selby

Contact: Jselby@twinkletoesbook.com
Www.twinkletoesbook.com

ISBN: 9798838265067

All art and graphics by Daniel Maisonet.

Printed by KDP publishing via Amazon.

Deep in the woods

where nobody goes

There lives a fairy

named Twinkle Toes.

She flutters about,

dancing on leaves

I wonder what she has

With a sprinkle of fairy dust

She makes flowers bloom

all around the pond.

Daffodils & Roses

The smell of the flowers

The time has come

for the sun to se

Twinkle toes flutters home

to get some rest.

More flowers to bloom,

more fairy dust to spread.

Goodnight, Twinkle Toes!

A nurse practitioner by day, a dreamer by night, Jennifer Selby is an imagination enthusiast, hoping to keep the magic within us alive through children's books.

An artist by trade, a philosopher by curiosity, Daniel Maisonet is an enthusiastic, multi-faceted creative with a penchant to bring fantastical worlds into a visual reality.

Raised in Newburgh, NY, Jen and Dan have been friends since highschool. When Twinkle Toes was created, Jen knew there was no one else who could make what was in her head, come alive on paper. Working full time jobs, juggling family and friends, even living on opposite ends of the country did not stop this dynamic duo from completing this magical journey. We hope you loved it as much as we do :).

Made in the USA
Middletown, DE
24 July 2022